Sally was not a new spinning wheel. Mrs. King had brought her home five years ago, when Sally's last owner had died. But Sally was in good shape. She didn't squeak and scratch when she spun. Mrs. King kept her very well dusted.

"I've heard about these new knitting machines," Sally said. "My friend Elmo was talking about them at the spinning-wheel convention last year. He knew ten spinning wheels that couldn't keep up with the new knitting machines. I didn't really listen to him, but maybe he was right. Maybe I won't be able to keep up with a knitting machine!"

Sally thought for a minute.

"You know, these knitting machines can work day and night because they're powered by electricity," she said. "They never get tired. I *won't* be able to keep up!"

"Don't get upset, Sally," Ned replied. "Let's wait and see what Mrs. King says. There's probably nothing to worry about."

"You're right, Ned," said Sally. "And those machines do make an awful noise. I can't believe Mrs. King would want one! There must be some mistake."

Ned stretched up to the window again, to see what was happening. He nearly popped out his bristles!

"Well, you'll find out soon, Sally," said Ned. "Here they come!"

The New Machine

Sally watched the door. She told herself not to worry.

"Maybe the new knitting machine and I will be friends," she thought. "It does get a bit lonely in here when Ned's out sweeping the rest of the house. It might be nice to have someone else to talk to."

Mrs. King and the driver of the truck came into the room. The truck driver was carrying a large box. The box looked heavy.

The driver put the box on the table and left. Mrs. King opened it excitedly.

"I know what you're thinking, Sally, but you don't need to worry," said Mrs. King. "Natalie Knitter is going to make your yarn into sweaters for me. There will be even more work for you now!"

Mrs. King lifted a gleaming white machine out of the box.

Natalie Knitter, the new knitting machine, was so shiny that she dazzled Sally. Mrs. King plugged in Natalie and switched her on.

Natalie's lights blinked. She made whirring and clicking sounds.

"Who are you?" Natalie asked Sally, in a very high voice. "And what is such an ugly spinning wheel doing in my new home?"

"Now, Natalie," said Mrs. King, "that's no way to talk to your new friend. This is Sally, Sally Spinner. Sally, meet Natalie Knitter."

Sally looked at Natalie. Natalie looked away.

"Nice to meet you," said Sally.

But Natalie said nothing at all.

"Oh no," thought Sally. "This is going to be even worse than I thought!"

"Right," said Mrs. King. "Come along, Ned, the kitchen floors are looking a bit dirty. We've got work to do."

Ned smiled at Sally as he followed Mrs. King out the door.

"I won't be friendly," thought Sally. "Natalie is a rude, nasty knitting machine!"

"Well, Sally," said Natalie, "Mrs. King will soon find out that you can't keep up with me! She'll get rid of you and buy yarn instead. But I can be kind to you until then, I suppose."

Sally felt her spokes begin to jangle. This was a bad sign. It only happened when she was very grumpy.

"Look, Miss Stuck-Up Knitter, I don't know what kind of spinning wheels you're used to working with, but I can spin as well as any spinning wheel! And I can spin a lot better than a machine that needs electricity to work!" said Sally. "What's so wonderful about knitting machines, anyway?"

Natalie laughed.

"Well, we'll see, won't we?" she said. "I bet you'll be retired by the end of the week. I'm the very latest knitter, you know. I can turn yarn into sweaters faster than you can say *silly old spinning wheel*!"

Then she turned her back on Sally. Her lights winked on and off as if they were laughing at Sally, too.

"If you're going to be nasty," thought Sally, "I'll show you!"

For the rest of the day Sally spun and spun. She worked from ten in the morning until ten that night. By the time she had finished, there was a huge pile of yarn. It was ready and waiting for Natalie to start work on the next day.

"Let's see how fast Natalie knits through that big pile of yarn," thought Sally.

Then she fell asleep, worn out.

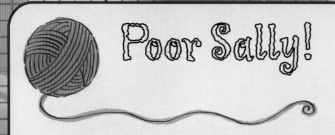

Poor Sally!

Sally woke early next morning to a whirring sound. She stretched, and looked over to where Natalie was knitting busily.

Sally couldn't believe her eyes! The huge pile of yarn that had taken her a whole day to spin was nearly finished! And Natalie was whizzing along so quickly, the yarn was going to be finished before Mrs. King even got out of bed this morning!

"Oh well," thought Sally. "I suppose I'll just have to work twice as hard today. I'll show that Natalie Knitter! Mrs. King won't get rid of me! But oh dear, I still feel so sleepy!"

Sally took a deep breath and went to work. Her wheel spun and spun. Her pedal went faster and faster.

"Be careful, you silly old spinning wheel," said Natalie, "you might hurt yourself!"

Sally didn't hear her. She spun even faster. Smoke started to pour out of her wheel. She felt dizzy.

Mrs. King rushed into the room.

"I can smell smoke!" she said.

Then she saw Sally. Sally was on fire!

"I'll get some water!" shouted Mrs. King, and she rushed out again.

Mrs. King came back with a bucket of water. She threw the cold water over Sally, while Sally coughed and choked. There were clouds of smoke in the room.

"That was the funniest thing I've ever seen," Natalie said, laughing.

"Be quiet, Natalie," said Mrs. King, "or I'll put you back in your box!"

Natalie stopped giggling.

"I'm sorry, Mrs. King," said Sally, nearly crying. "I was trying to go fast to keep up with Natalie. Maybe she's right. Maybe I am just a silly old spinning wheel."

Tears spilled down Sally's spokes and onto the wet floor.

"I'm sorry that Natalie has made you feel sad," said Mrs. King. "But it was a bit silly to start a fire!"

"I didn't mean to," Sally said. "What's going to happen to me now?"

"Well, you've burned your spokes," said Mrs. King. "I'm not sure you'll ever be able to spin yarn again."

Sally cried even harder. Then Ned swept in from the kitchen.

"What's been going on here?" he asked. "This room needs a mop, not a broom! Open the window and let the smoke out, Mrs. King. What's happened to you, Sally? Why are you crying?"

"Oh Ned," sobbed Sally. "I've burned my spokes trying to keep up with Natalie! And Mrs. King doesn't think I'll ever be able to spin again!"

She sobbed even more loudly.

"I've got an idea," said Ned. "Why don't you go and see Mr. Dumbleton, the woodworker? When Fred, the yard broom, was hurt, Mr. King took him along to Mr. Dumbleton. Mr. Dumbleton made Fred as good as new."

"What a good idea, Ned," said Mrs. King. "I didn't think of Mr. Dumbleton! We'll send Sally there! Cheer up, Sally, you'll be fine in no time."

The Dumbletons

Mr. Dumbleton arrived to pick up Sally an hour later. He told Mrs. King he'd have her back in a few days. When he got home, he took Sally to his workshop, and went straight to work.

"Don't worry, I'll have you back in shape in no time," Mr. Dumbleton said to Sally.

Sally almost fell asleep as Mr. Dumbleton replaced her burned spokes. Then he sanded and he oiled and he polished. And when she thought he was about to stop, he oiled and he polished some more. She started to feel like a new spinning wheel.

"There you go, Sally Spinner," he said, at last. "You're as good as new again."

He put Sally in the sun, and he started to work on a table that had lost a leg.

Late in the afternoon, Mrs. Dumbleton came out to the workshop to talk to Mr. Dumbleton. When she saw Sally sitting in the sun, she got very excited.

"My grandmother had a spinning wheel just like this one!" she said. "That spinning wheel spun the softest yarn I've ever felt. Her name was Sally, I think, Sally Spinner. I've always wondered what happened to her after Grandma died."

Sally became wide awake. She turned and looked at Mrs. Dumbleton.

"I remember you! You're Gretchen!" Sally exclaimed. "Gretchen Glossop! Your grandma used to knit you sweaters with the yarn I spun!"

"Well, I've been Gretchen Dumbleton for the last ten years," said Mrs. Dumbleton, "ever since I married Mr. Dumbleton. I can't believe it's you, Sally Spinner. What happened to you?"

"When your grandma died, I was sold," said Sally. "Mrs. King has been taking good care of me, but she's bought a new knitting machine, and I just can't keep up."

Mr. Dumbleton heard their voices, and came out of his workshop to find out what was happening.

"I mustn't lose Sally again," said Mrs. Dumbleton to her husband. "Let's go and ask Mrs. King if Sally can stay with us."

They got ready to set off to see Mrs. King.

"One more thing," called Sally. "My friend Ned lives with Mrs. King, too. Could you please let him know what has happened? Otherwise he'll worry about me."

"Of course we will," said Mrs. Dumbleton. "We'll tell your friend Ned that you'll be happy here."

Mr. and Mrs. Dumbleton came back quite soon. Ned was with them!

"Hi Sally!" said Ned. "Natalie Knitter convinced Mrs. King to buy a vacuum cleaner. She didn't need me anymore either! She was very pleased that we've both found such a good home."

"This has all worked out perfectly," said Sally, smiling.

But Ned didn't answer. He'd already found some dirt on the floor. He was busy, sweeping it away.

A Happy Ending

"Come on, Sally," said Mrs. Dumbleton. "I can't wait to see if your yarn is as good as it used to be!"

Sally felt very nervous. What if Mr. Dumbleton hadn't repaired her properly? What if the fire had damaged her spokes for good? Maybe Mrs. Dumbleton wouldn't want to keep her after all.

Mrs. Dumbleton gave Sally some wool to spin. Sally got to work, spinning the wool quickly. Then she held her breath as Mrs. Dumbleton felt the yarn she had spun. Was it good enough?

"Oh Sally, this yarn is perfect! It's just as soft as I remember," said Mrs. Dumbleton.

So Sally went on spinning happily. She would have a wonderful story to tell at the next spinning-wheel convention!